Dear Parent:
Your child's love of reading starts here!

Every child learns to read in a different way and at his or her own speed. Some go back and forth between reading levels and read favorite books again and again. Others read through each level in order. You can help your young reader improve and become more confident by abilities. From books your c or she reads alone, there a eading:

My First **SHA** Basic illustrations, ideal

1 **BEG** Shor ncepts for c

2 **REA** Enga e play for d

3 **REA** Com h-interest topics for t

4 **ADV** Shor es for t

I Can Read joy of reading since 1957. F ators and a fabulous cast set the standard for

A lifetime of discovery begins with the magical words **"I Can Read!"**

Visit www.icanread.com for information on enriching your child's reading experience.

ISBN 978-0-545-86459-6

Published by Scholastic Inc., 557 Broadway, New York, NY 10012, by arrangement with HarperCollins Children's Books,
a division of HarperCollins Publishers.

18 17 16 15 18 19 20/0

Printed in the U.S.A. 40

First Scholastic printing, September 2015

Pete the Cat

A Pet for Pete

By James Dean

SCHOLASTIC INC.

Pete is going to the pet store.
He is going to get a pet.
Pete wants a bird,
a hamster, or a lizard.

But then Pete sees a goldfish.
“That’s what I want,”
he tells his mom.

Pete's mom gets fish food.
"I'm going to call you Goldie,"
Pete says to his new pet.

"You are my first pet,"
Pete tells Goldie
on the way home.

Pete takes Goldie to his room.
He feeds her fish food.
"Now what?" asks Pete.

He can’t play with Goldie.
He can’t swim with her.
Pete knows what he can do!

Pete paints a picture of Goldie.
He paints four fins
and an orange tail.

“What a pretty painting,”
says Pete’s mom.
“You can keep it,” says Pete.

“Cool painting!” says Bob.
“Can you make one for me?”
“Sure,” says Pete.

Pete paints a picture for Bob.

“Wow!” says Bob.

“It looks just like Goldie.”

Bob shows Pete's painting
to his friend Tom.
Now Tom wants a painting, too.

Pete paints another picture of Goldie to take to school for show-and-tell.

“This is Goldie, my pet fish,”
Pete tells his class.

"Cute fish!"
"Cool colors!"
"Nice work!"

"I wish I had a picture
of Goldie," says Benny.
"I'll make you one," says Pete.

Everyone in Pete's class
wants a painting of Goldie!

Pete's grandma wants
a painting, too.

Pete has a lot to do.
He has to feed Goldie.
He has to do homework.

Pete paints and paints.
He makes paintings for
everyone on his list.

At last Pete is done!

He worked hard.

There is no paint left.

Pete's paintings are a big hit!

Pete is happy to be done.

But Pete is not done.
Now everyone in town
wants a painting of Goldie!

Pete gets more paint.
"I don't know what to do,"
he says to his mom.

"I wish I could paint
pictures for everyone.
I just don't have time."

Pete's mom has an idea!

She tells it to Pete.

"Great idea!" says Pete.

Pete gets right to it.
This time he works outside
and makes a huge painting.

Honk! Honk!

Beep! Beep!

Here comes Pete!

He has made one painting

of Goldie for everyone

in town to enjoy!

What a great day!
When Pete gets home, he tells the real Goldie all about it.